ELLEN CUTLER

ELLEN CUTLER

A VISIT TO THE

Art Galaxy

BY
ANNIE REINER

GREEN TIGER PRESS, INC.

Green Tiger Press, Inc.
435 East Carmel Street, San Marcos, CA 92069
First Edition
1 3 5 7 9 10 8 6 4 2
Library of Congress Catalog Card Number: 90-61402
ISBN: 0–88138–151–9

I would like to thank
Carole Ita White
for bringing this idea to my attention;
Charlotte Gusay
for her unyielding faith and tireless efforts
in getting the book published.
I am grateful to Bernard Bail
for the knowledge of
what it really means to be a child.

For Lorraine Gorlick

On a beautiful Saturday morning, Peter and Bess could think of plenty of things they'd rather do than go to the art museum. Bess wanted to play with her new puppy, and Peter wanted to play ball with his friends.

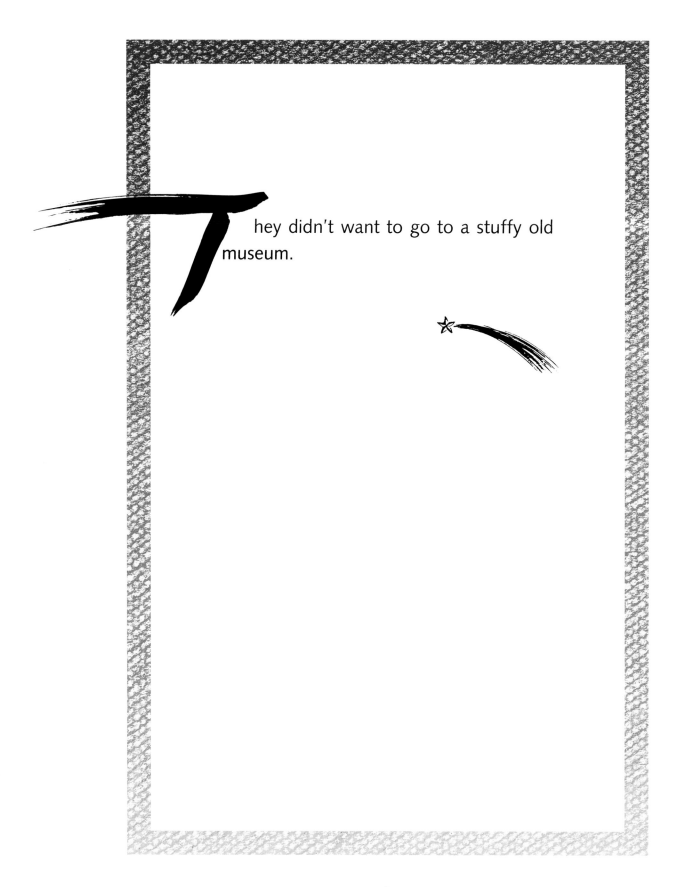

They didn't want to go to a stuffy old museum.

I don't even know what modern art is,'' Peter grumbled, walking up the steps of the museum.

''It's art that is new. You'll like it, you'll see,'' their mother said, noticing their sad, reluctant faces.

Inside the museum, it was very quiet, like a library or a church, and the walls were filled, hung with colorful pictures.

Peter and Bess looked at the first picture on the wall, but didn't know what it was — just three colors: a block of dark purple, a big block of black on top, and a brown stripe running right across the middle. Their mother left to look at another painting while the two children stared at the mysterious picture.

"What is it?" Peter asked his sister.

Bess didn't answer. Something strange had begun to happen to her eyes. She had never seen a black so black, glowing like clouds in a night sky. She felt dizzy, as if she were flying!

lancing down, she saw that her feet
had left the floor. She really was flying!
Bess flew right into the picture, but not
before she grabbed her brother's hand and
he came flying along after her.

The painting became a spaceship that carried them away into the sky.

This was no ordinary sky, for in it all sorts of objects danced. Amidst the swirling stars, they saw a vase of pretty flowers and a bowl of bright, delicious fruit.

A white-haired man appeared out of nowhere with a little white pigeon perched upon his shoulder. He painted a picture of the fruit and flowers that whirled past Bess' and Peter's eyes.

W ho are you?'' Peter called.

"I'm Monsieur Matisse," he said. "Welcome to the Land Of Modern Art."

"Is that where we are?" the children asked.

"Yes, of course. Where are your paints and brushes?"

"We don't have any paints."

"Well, most people come here to paint," Matisse said, "but never mind. Welcome!"

Monsieur Matisse turned, waving to an old man who floated by wearing a long tunic. "Hello, Leonardo," he called.

"Who's he?" Bess asked.

e is the great master, Leonardo da Vinci."

"He doesn't look so modern to me," Peter remarked, eyeing his old fashioned clothes and long flowing beard. "I thought this was the Land Of Modern Art."

"It is," Matisse explained, "maybe Leonardo is not a modern artist of *your* day, but he was modern in *his* day, even though it was such a long time ago. Styles change, but artists throughout history have always come here to paint."

*W*hy?" the children asked.

"Because there's so much room to dream," he said. "And as you see, things look different up here." He showed them his finished picture.

"Those don't look much like apples to me," Peter said.

"Ah, but they look like apples to *me*," Matisse exclaimed. "I paint what apples taste like, that's why my apples look like this. I guess they taste different to everyone. What do your apples taste like?"

*B*ess thought about the sweet juice of an apple in her mouth, and different colors flashed inside her mind like brilliant stars.

"Pink and yellow and red!" she called out to Matisse.

"Wonderful, wonderful! I can hardly wait to see them."

"But we don't have any paints," Bess said.

"Oh yes, that *is* a problem," Matisse admitted. Without offering a solution, the old man disappeared.

A puffy blue cloud surrounded the spaceship and Peter and Bess couldn't see a thing. When it cleared, they saw a picture of a silly looking woman, which made them laugh.

"Go ahead, laugh!" Another man appeared. "I am Picasso," he said, his dark eyes flashing, "and you are not the first to laugh at my work. But who cares! I paint what I like, what I see…things moving, always moving. Up here, there are a lot of ways to look at things. Not just one."

With that, Picasso vanished, his painting was left floating before them.

The lady in Picasso's painting had a gigantic nose and her eyes were not quite right. One of them was stuck on her nose! Peter said, "It reminds me of Mommy's face right up close when she kisses me goodnight. Sometimes her eyes are right on top of each other, or she has two noses!"

But Picasso's picture made Bess think of dancing, and with a joyous leap she sprang from the
spaceship to dance freely in the wide-open space.
"Whee-ee-ee!" she squealed with such delight
that Peter joined her.

Giggling, Bess watched her brother whirl around and around, looking just like Picasso's painting, with his nose sliding around to his ear and his eyes whizzing all over his face as he turned. They both laughed and laughed, and saw that Picasso was right. Up here, there were a lot of ways to see things.

It was fun dancing in the sky, but their spaceship had floated away. They drifted along in the silence of space for an awfully long time, until finally, far in the distance, they saw a group of people.

t least they thought they were people, but, moving closer, what they saw were statues, taller and skinnier than any real people could ever be.

"Like shadows," Peter whispered to his sister, "shadows which grow taller and taller in the moonlight and seem to follow you down the street." Both children shuddered, as chills ran up their spines. What would happen if the shadows of the night became real?

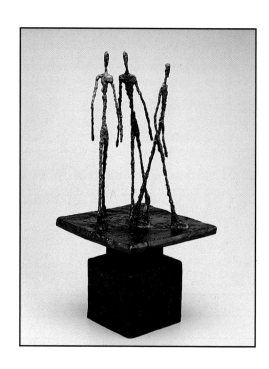

Safely past the statues, a new kind of painting appeared, without any people in it, or fruit or flowers — it didn't even have any colors, just splashes of black paint which a man made in grand, sweeping gestures onto a white canvas.

"Hello! Hello!" they called out, glad to see a person again. He said his name was Franz Kline. "What are you doing?" Bess asked.

am painting shadows come to life," the man said mysteriously. "They are shadows of thoughts, shadows of feelings, shadows of things I have seen."

Peter and Bess didn't understand, and like a shadow, Franz Kline disappeared before they could ask what he meant. Looking at his picture, they couldn't make any sense of the design.

ut then it seemed to spring to life, and a big, black bull stomped his feet and charged right at them!

Swept onto his back, he carried the children away, flying across the sky. They were flying so fast …

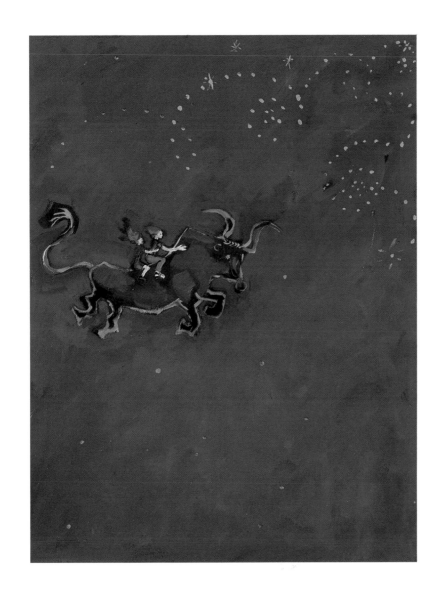

… that they tumbled off and went rolling and spinning, laughing through the stars. The bull galloped off, becoming just a tiny dot in the sky. He looked like a star high above, winking down with a fiery eye.

Wow!"

"Art sure is different up here."

The children began to worry about being so far away from home. They couldn't figure out how to go back when they didn't know how they got up there in the first place. They wanted to see their mother, and called out, "Mommy!" but instead of their mother, Monsieur Matisse appeared. He carried paints and brushes and two big canvasses.

"Maybe now you are ready to paint a picture too," he said.

"We don't want to paint," Peter said. "We just want to go home."

"Please help us!" Bess pleaded.

"I will leave you these magic paints," he offered.

"What's magic about them?"

"Well actually, all paints are magic in the Land Of Modern Art," Matisse confided. "Have fun!"

un?'' Bess said. ''But I'm hungry, and tired.''

''And scared,'' Peter added. But by then Monsieur Matisse was gone. The children were all alone.

''Oh no, now we're really lost,'' Peter said. But they were curious about the magic paints, so many pretty colors.

Like Franz Kline, Bess picked up a brush and made a big red splash. Peter dipped his brush in blue paint and splattered his canvas. The colors swirled before their eyes — red, yellow, blue —

And before they knew it, each had painted a picture of their house. Of course, they looked entirely different, because up in the Land Of Modern Art there was so much room to dream.

*B*ess painted their mother standing right out in front. But it was only a picture. How would they get home? As Peter finished painting their big Saint Bernard in the front yard, a young man appeared before them. He said his name was Chris Burden.

"How do you like my work of art?" he asked.

They looked around but didn't see any pictures. They didn't see any sculptures, or see anything at all until the man pointed to a hole in the sky.

*T*hat's art?'' Peter asked.

As they moved closer, they saw that it was a flight of stairs, but it wasn't any kind of art they knew about.

''Certainly it's art,'' the man explained. ''Art can be anything that helps you to dream your own dreams, or bring you new dreams,'' he said.

They examined his work after he disappeared. ''It still looks like steep stairs to me,'' Peter said. ''What's a staircase doing in the sky?''

''Let's find out,'' Bess sugggested.

Clutching each other's hands, they walked slowly down the stairs. Bess stopped, "Uh-oh, I can't feel the next step."

"If we turn back now, we may never get home," Peter said, and so they kept on going. But Bess was right, there were no more steps! The children tumbled down, down and down ...

"Help!" Peter called, falling, as shivers ran down his spine, all the way to his toes. The children feared they would fall forever.

Something touched their shoulders. Wheeling around, they were astonished to see, standing there in front of them, their mother! Bess and Peter wrapped their arms around her in a great big hug.

O h, Mommy, are we happy to see you!"

"Did you enjoy the museum, children?"

"The museum?" Peter was confused. Sure enough, there was the big painting with purple and black blocks of color and a brown stripe in the middle.

"But, Mommy, we were in a spaceship, and then we were dancing!"

"And we rode on a bull until we fell off and he disappeared into the stars," Peter added, "and there were artists painting, and we painted pictures, too, with magic paint."

"What imaginations you have!"

"No, Mom, it was real."

Their mother did not appear convinced.

"Well," Bess said, remembering what she learned in the Land Of Modern Art, "I guess there are a lot of ways to look at things. Not just one."

T hat's right," their mother said, surprised. "But where did you learn that?"

Bess and Peter glanced again at the dark painting with the glowing sky, then looked at each other knowingly, and smiled.

The text of this book was set in Syntax
by TypeLink of San Diego, California

Interior and cover design and hand lettering
by Eileen Boniecka & James Nocito of Persimmon Graphics

Text edited by Lynne T. Harwich and Brian Hutchins

Printing and binding by Lake Book Manufacturing, Inc.,
Melrose Park, Illinois

Photography by Grey Crawford